Jim's Dog Muffins

STORY BY
MIRIAM COHEN

PICTURES BY
LILLIAN HOBAN

A Picture Yearling Book

Published by
Bantam Doubleday Dell Books for Young Readers
a division of
Bantam Doubleday Dell Publishing Group, Inc.
1540 Broadway
New York, New York 10036

ISBN: 0-440-41124-6
Reprinted by arrangement with Greenwillow Books, a division of William Morrow & Company, Inc.

Printed in the United States of America

July 1996
10 9 8 7 6 5 4 3 2 1

FOR DR. EDITH WEIGERT—

"NATURE WILL SAY,

'DON'T CRY ANYMORE.'"

"Jim's dog got killed by the garbage truck!
It was all squashed!
Jim's not coming to school today."
Danny was telling everybody about it.

"Did Jim cry?" Paul asked.

"No," Danny said. "But he wouldn't talk to anybody."

Their teacher said, "Jim must be very sad.
If we write a letter to him,
it might help him feel better."

The teacher wrote what they said.

After school, the teacher took the letter to Jim's house.

When Jim came back, he wouldn't talk to anybody.
That morning they gave their whale reports.
Louie said, "Whales will never bite you."

And Paul said that whales can even sing.
But Jim wasn't listening.
He was thinking about Muffins.

The home-making teacher came in with bags of carrots, onions, parsley, and potatoes. "We're going to cook vegetable soup today." She showed them how to cut up everything into small pieces.

Anna Maria said, "Danny is throwing big pieces in!" Everybody was waiting for the soup to be cooked, except Jim. He was looking out the window.

When the soup was ready, they invited the principal to have lunch with them. They sat down at the table and the principal and the teacher started to eat. "Oh, this is so good!" they said.

But Danny said, "There is something in here!
What is it? Yech! Parsley!"
And he began to take every piece of parsley
out of his soup. By the time he got it all out,
lunch was over.

In the playground, Jim sat on a bench.
Louie and Sammy came over to see him.
"Maybe you'll forget Muffins, Jim?"
Jim shook his head.

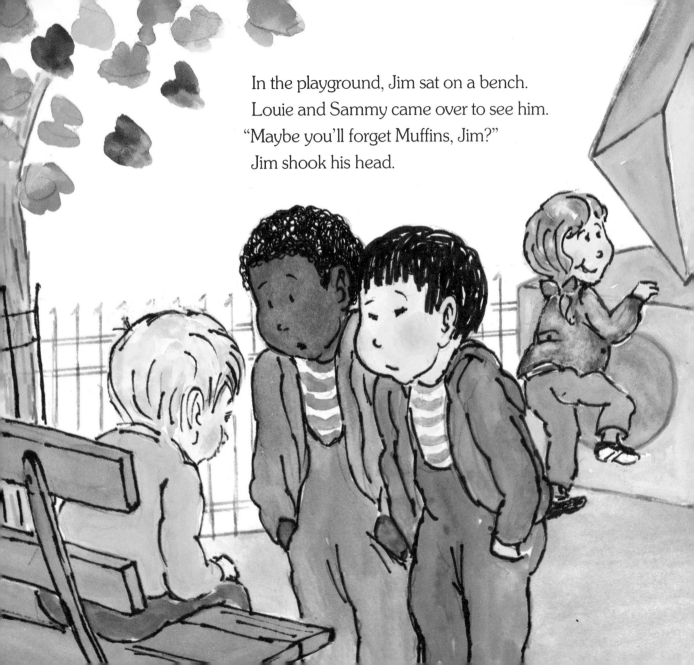

Danny put his arm around Jim.
"Don't worry," he said. "I'm never going to die."
Jim didn't say anything.

Anna Maria sat down on
the bench next to Jim.
"It doesn't do any good
to be sad," she said.

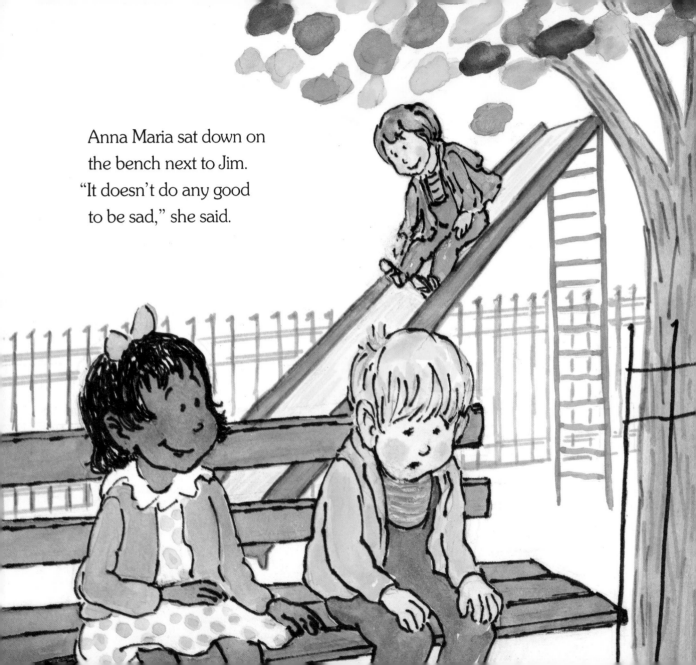

Jim yelled, "Shut up! Get away!"
And he pushed Anna Maria off the bench.

Anna Maria started screaming. When
the teacher came, she cried, "I was
just trying to make him feel better!"

The teacher said,
"Maybe Jim needs time
to feel sad."

Jim stayed by himself. If anybody came near,
he put his hands on his ears.
And Anna Maria told them, "Don't play with him."

Jim didn't even choose a book
when it was time for the whole
school to stop and read. He just sat.

After school Jim
started home again.

Paul ran after him. "My father gave me money for two slices of pizza. Come on, Jim."

"I don't want any," Jim said.

The pizza smell came around the corner.
When they came to the store, Paul stopped.
"Two slices please," he said.

He gave one to Jim.
Jim just held it.
Then Paul did what they always did.
He pushed a lot of pizza into his mouth.

Jim looked at Paul. He took one bite.
Then he began pushing pizza in.
They began to laugh.
They laughed and laughed.

Jim said, "Remember how I used to give Muffins the crust?"
Tears came down on his pizza, but he kept on eating.

"She was the nicest dog,"
  Paul said.
"Yes," said Jim.
  And they walked home together.